Journey to a New Land

The Mayflower
by Kersten

Joëlle Murphy

Illustrated by John Fairbridge and Mark Payne

Rigby

Our class is learning what it was like to sail on the *Mayflower*.

We're finding out lots of things. We're writing a Pilgrim's diary about the journey.

September 6, 1620

There are **102** people on the Mayflower. **34** of us are children and I am one of them. We are going to the New World! I am a little bit scared...

The *Mayflower* set sail for the New World on September 6, 1620.

The *Mayflower* was very crowded. The Pilgrims spent most of their time "between decks."

September 29, 1620

We've been at sea now for 24 days. I am tired of eating the same food every day. We can't wash our clothes or take a bath.

During storms, the *Mayflower's* sails were pulled up so the ship wouldn't be blown off course.

A model of the Mayflower
by Molly

October 8, 1620

The storm has been blowing for three days now. I fear a wave might break the ship in two! Will the wind ever stop howling? Will we ever see the New World?

The sailor on lookout was
the first to see land.

November 9, 1620

Land ho! It has taken us 65 days to reach the New World! I can't wait to get off this ship and walk on dry land.

The Pilgrims lived on the *Mayflower* during the first winter. They came ashore most days to build their houses.

January 11, 1621

There are bad storms. The wind is blowing strongly and the land is covered with ice. Many people are ill. We're staying on the ship until our houses are built. But how can we build our houses with so many people sick?

Samoset was the first Native American
to become friends with the Pilgrims.

Native Americans taught the Pilgrims how to:

Fish

Hunt

Gather Clams and Mussels

Plant Corn

Displayed by James

March 16, 1621

I met an Indian today! His name is Samoset. He spoke English! He told us about another Indian named Squanto. Squanto speaks English, too. Squanto will help us in this new land.

Pilgrims and Native Americans joined together for the first Thanksgiving.

October 14, 1621

We have worked hard! Today is the beginning of a great celebration. We are gathering with the Indians today to give thanks for a good harvest and a strong friendship. We have much to be thankful for.

Our class learned a lot about Pilgrims. Now
when we celebrate Thanksgiving, we really feel
like we're the children of Pilgrims.